COLOUR JETS

Dear Alien

Angie Sage

Collins

KT-557-265

COLOUR JETS

First published in paperback in Great Britain by
HarperCollins*Publishers* Ltd 1998

The HarperCollins website address is
www.**fire**and**water**.com

12 11 10 9 8 7 6 5 4 3

Text and illustrations © Angie Sage 1998

The author/illustrator asserts the moral right to be
identified as the author/illustrator of the work.

A CIP record for this title is available
from the British Library.

ISBN 0 00 675340 X

Printed in Hong Kong

Chapter 1

It all started when Miss Fowler got out a list of pen friends.

> This term we are all going to write to a pen friend. We can find out how people in different places live.

Everybody in the class had to choose one.

It's not true that I can never make up my mind. Not true at all.

I mean, if I had to choose between keeping my brother or my gerbil, I'd go for the gerbil straight away. Easy.
But pen friends? Well, that's different.

4

"By tomorrow morning, Sam," said
Miss Fowler, "or I'll be expecting a
letter from you."

I walked home from school with Jaz and
Pete, but I didn't say much. I was too
busy wondering where I was going to
find a pen friend. Well, where do you find
a pen friend when you need one?

We got to the end of Jaz and Pete's road.

When I got home I still didn't have any ideas.

"You could write to Auntie Mabel," said Mum. "She likes writing letters. She'll tell you all about her cats."

Great.

"You could write to my bank manager," said Dad. "A bank is a very interesting place."

Yes, Dad.

Woof?

"You could write to ME!" said my brother. "I never get any letters."

"I'm not surprised," I told him. "You're not getting any from me, either."

Then the clock struck six.

ting
ting
ting
ting
ting
ting

Treehouse! I'm late!

Chapter 2

I was late, but not that late. When I got to the treehouse, no one was there…

Weird!

… but they had been. It looked like Jaz and Pete had left in a hurry. Jaz's baseball cap was on the floor, and Pete's bag was swinging from a branch.

Then I saw something shining. It was wedged in the corner of the treehouse window.

It looked like a multi-coloured chocolate wrapper, shimmering and flickering in hundreds of different colours.

I picked it up.

OUCH!

It was hot!

I dropped it at once.

The setting sun made strange shadows on the wrapper as it fluttered down to the floor.

I stared at them hard and they began to change.

They're words! It's a letter!

12

The shadows had
sort of melted into
words.

Dear Gril. Or Boy.

Please write
here your name
and age and
species for me.

From Luek

At first I thought Jaz and Pete must
be playing a trick on me. Maybe
they were hiding somewhere.
But the more I looked at the
chocolate wrapper, the more
it looked like a real letter.

"Hey," I thought, "I've got
a pen friend."

I fished out a pencil and paper from
Pete's bag and wrote back:

Dear Luke

I am not a girl I am a boy.
I am 8 years old and my
name is Sam.
will you be my pen friend?
what is your best food?
How old are you?

From Sam

PS Ha ha. what species!
very funny.

PPS Human.

I suddenly realised I didn't know where to post the letter, so I put it where I'd found the chocolate wrapper.

By then it was getting dark and the treehouse was beginning to feel a bit spooky.

I was sure I could hear a strange humming sound and the hairs on the back of my neck prickled.

I jumped down and ran home pretty fast. Not that I was scared or anything.

That night something woke me up.
A strange light was shining through the
curtains and I was sure I could hear
that humming sound again.

I just had to have a look, so I lifted up
the corner of the curtain.

The whole treehouse was
lit up by an eerie glow.

Wow!

For once I was glad to be safe
at home in boring old bed.

Chapter 3

The next morning I had something to tell Miss Fowler.

I've got a pen friend. I wrote a letter last night.

I looked for the chocolate wrapper, to show her, but it wasn't in my pocket. Just some coloured dust.

Miss Fowler didn't look impressed.

Where does your pen friend live, Sam?

Umm. I don't know yet.

I could see this did not sound too good.
I mean, how can you write to someone
if you don't know where they live?

I see, Sam.
You can write me a nice
letter this playtime. You can
send it to my desk, here.

Well, I've had
better playtimes,
I can tell you.

After school I caught up with Jaz and
Pete and gave them back their stuff.
I wanted to know why they'd gone off
without me last night.

Coming to the
treehouse?

No way!

It was turning out to be one of those
days. I asked them why not. They
looked a bit embarrassed, I thought.

We-ell... it's not
that we're scared
or anything...

But... that
treehouse is dead
weird, Sam.

And we're not going back. Byeee!

They disappeared down the road as if the treehouse itself was chasing them.

When I thought about it, I wasn't too happy about going to the treehouse either. But the trouble was, it was either the treehouse or writing to Miss Fowler.

Well, which would you choose?

But everything seemed fine when I got there. I climbed up the ladder and sat down on the warm planks. It was quiet and peaceful, and the little birdies were singing.

Tweety tweet!

And there was a letter!

Chapter 4

The letter was written on another coloured chocolate wrapper. It was warm and smelt like the back of our telly when it gets hot.

human
you
are
one!

Dear Sam,

I write you back!
This is good. My tutor
tell me to contact Human.
And I find you are one.
This is a good joke?

My best food is djoj →

and I am 10 cycles now for
we have travelled fast.

FAST
FAST   FAST

Do you have Human family
beings? Which ones?

Goodbye from Luek
(Not Luke. This is
very rude word.)

I carefully put the
letter in my schoolbag.
"That'll show Miss Fowler," I thought.

Dear Luek,

Can you make your letters a bit stronger? The last one fell to bits when I showed it to Miss Fowler and she got cross because all the pieces fell in her cup of coffee and made it fizz.

She is horrible. I hope your tutor is nicer than her.

In my family
there is my mum,

my dad,

my gran

and my brother,
but I don't think
he counts as human exactly.

It is my birthday soon.
I am having a party.

Love from Sam.

PS Are you an alien?

Dear Sam,

I am most sorry about this Fowler. What is a party? Tick box please.

What species is your brother?

Tick box please.

Love from Luek

PS I am not an Alien. You are.

Dear ... **Luck**

Please come to my birthday party

on ... **Tuesday**

from ... **5.30** ... to ... **8.00**

Reply: I can come

          I cannot come

From: ....

Reply: ~~I can come~~

           I cannot come

           ....

From: Luek......................

Dear Sam,

I cannot come because my tutor is cross. He is just like the Fowler. He tells me I am not finished my project on Human so I must stay in the Mother Ship.

He say my project is not good and he may not let me go echo-chasing on Kren. This is sad.

Love from Luek

PS
I access birthday
and I find you have
present giving as
we do. So I send
present. Also I say
Happy Birthday To You.

Love from
Luek

To
Sam
x

I was really disappointed that Luek couldn't come to my party, but the present was BRILLIANT!
…Whatever it was…

Dear Luek,

Thank you lots and lots and LOTS for my present. What is it? Is it a space watch? I am wearing it now. It is just like star trek.

I am sorry about your tutor. He sounds as bad as Miss Fowler.

Love from Sam

PS what is echo-chasing?

Chapter 5

I put Luek's letter in my bag and walked to school very slowly. The teleport bracelet was sitting on my wrist blinking little red and green lights every now and then. I pulled my jumper sleeve down over it, but you could still see it.

Miss Fowler is going to go mad...

I bumped into Jaz and Pete and they spotted it straight away.

Hey, what's that?

You wearing your mum's bracelet?

NO WAY!

So, for the first lesson I sat on my hands.

At playtime I stuffed them in my pockets.

But it all went wrong when we had to draw a picture of our pen friends. The trouble was, Miss Fowler still thought *she* was my pen friend. She didn't believe a word I told her about Luek.

Come on, Sam. I'll pose for you.

She gave a daft smile, patted her hair and sat down in front of me. I was trapped!

I slowly got out my pencil and paper. The teleport bracelet blinked green. Miss Fowler's beady eyes stared at my wrist.

"No jewellery in school, Sam," she tutted. The class giggled.

The bracelet blinked red. Miss Fowler's eyes flashed.

I didn't want the teleport bracelet to get wet – I thought it might blow up or something. So when Miss Fowler loomed up waving a bar of soap, I quickly pulled my wrist away.

But she was quicker! She grabbed the bracelet and twisted it. The little red and green lights flashed faster and faster. Then a swirl of coloured stars flew out.

For a second I could see
Miss Fowler still hanging on to
my wrist, then the stars spun us
round and round. I felt as if I was being
s t r e t c h e d   o u t into little pieces
and then put back together again.

I closed my eyes.

43

When I opened them, we were on a spaceship. I just knew it had to be Luek's Mother Ship.

Welcome!
You Sam!
I Luek

I thought Miss Fowler would be pleased to meet my pen friend. At least now she would believe that I had one!

So I introduced her.

Miss Fowler – *this is* my pen friend, Luek.

She was really rude! She screamed!

In fact, she wouldn't stop screaming.
A spotty alien tried to talk to her, but it
only made her scream louder.

I put my hands over my ears.
The aliens held their flippers on
top of their heads, so I guessed
where *their*
ears were.

45

Luek sort of smiled at me and said,
"I show you Mother Ship, Sam. Yes?"

Well, I had to say "yes". After all, Miss
Fowler wanted us to find out how our
pen friends lived, didn't she? So I left her
screaming at the aliens and followed Luek.

The Mother Ship was like all the space
ships you have ever seen on the telly.
Brilliant.

Luek showed me the food machine…

The sleeping decks…

…until the spotty alien appeared and switched the gravity back on.

It was Luek's tutor.

How many times I tell you NOT to switch off gravity, Luek?

Whoooomp!

He was as bad as Miss Fowler!

Thud!

Boing!

He stood by the door with what I was sure was a silly smile on his face. Then I noticed Miss Fowler was with him. She'd stopped screaming, but she didn't look - you know - with it.

I talk to the lovely Fowler. She need some fun. We all go to Kren. We will echo-chase.

Hooooora!!!!

Miss Fowler... echo-chase???

Chapter 6

Miss Fowler went echo-chasing with us.
She did!

Luek's tutor pushed her into the Bug and
slammed the hatch quick before she
could get out again.

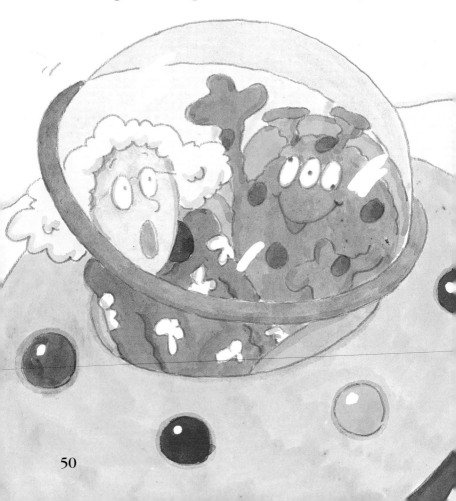

Jumps are weird. Everything goes
white and your head feels like jelly.
But before I had a chance to wonder
if I was going to be sick, we arrived.
Our Bug zoomed down towards the
towering Kren cliffs and hovered.

51

The Kren caves were massive.
Luek lined the Bug up outside one
that glowed purple.

"Good echoes here," he said. I looked
out of the cockpit and saw Miss Fowler
and Luek's tutor in their Bug. I was sure
Miss Fowler's hair was standing on end.

"Now we wait for echo," said Luek.

Suddenly there was a pleep!
and we were off.

Oooohh!

Luek grabbed the
control stick and we
swooped in behind
the echo.

OoooooAAAAAAH!

"Missed,"
said Luek.
"We get next one."

And we did. We got the next one, or it got us. It felt like the biggest corkscrew ride, trampoline and helter-skelter you have ever been on, all at the same time. It was AMAZING.

Your turn, Sam.

I took the control stick and waited for the pleep of an echo. And guess what? I caught it. First time! Just call me Space Bug Pilot from now on.

Suddenly the Bug with Luek's tutor in it flashed past us. It was chasing a really big echo.

But the tutor wasn't flying it.

It was Miss Fowler!

SWISHHHH

When we got back to the Mother Ship,
Miss Fowler and Luek's tutor were sitting
in the alien cafe. Miss Fowler was giggling.

Luek and I left them to it. It was time to go anyway. I felt sad, but Luek had a really good idea.

You come camping with me soon? We go to Vrall Valley.

Great!

Then he showed me how to work the teleport bracelet properly, so I could use it whenever I wanted. I set it for the treehouse and twisted…

Byeee!

Chapter 7

It was just my luck to find my brother hanging around when I climbed down the treehouse ladder.

Where have you been?

In space, if you must know.

"Oh, ha ha!" he giggled. "I know you weren't at school. You've been asleep in the treehouse. Wait till I tell Mum!"

I jumped down off the ladder. "Don't be daft," I told him.

He just danced off, singing at the top of his voice.

> Sam's been snoring in the treehouse. Naa-na na na-naaaah!

"Stupid boy," I thought. Then I thought again. Suppose he was right? Suppose I had been asleep in the treehouse all day?

I looked at the bracelet on my wrist, but it didn't give me any answers.

The next morning I didn't want to go to school.

Problem number one was, where exactly had I been yesterday? And what was I going to say to Miss Fowler?

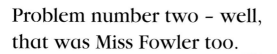

Problem number two – well, that was Miss Fowler too.

How did she get off the Mother Ship?

Was she ever on the Mother Ship?

Was I ever on the Mother Ship?

I bet I'll have to write her another letter.

Miss Fowler was in the playground when I got to school. She pounced on me at once.

And how's Sam today? How's your pen friend?

Er, fine, thank you, Miss Fowler.

Then she skipped off with a weird smile on her face.

Oh what a beautiful morn-ING...

It wasn't until the end of the day that I knew for certain I hadn't been dreaming.

"I certainly will," she grinned.

Something flashed red and green on her wrist. Miss Fowler twisted her teleport bracelet and, in a swirl of coloured stars, she was gone.